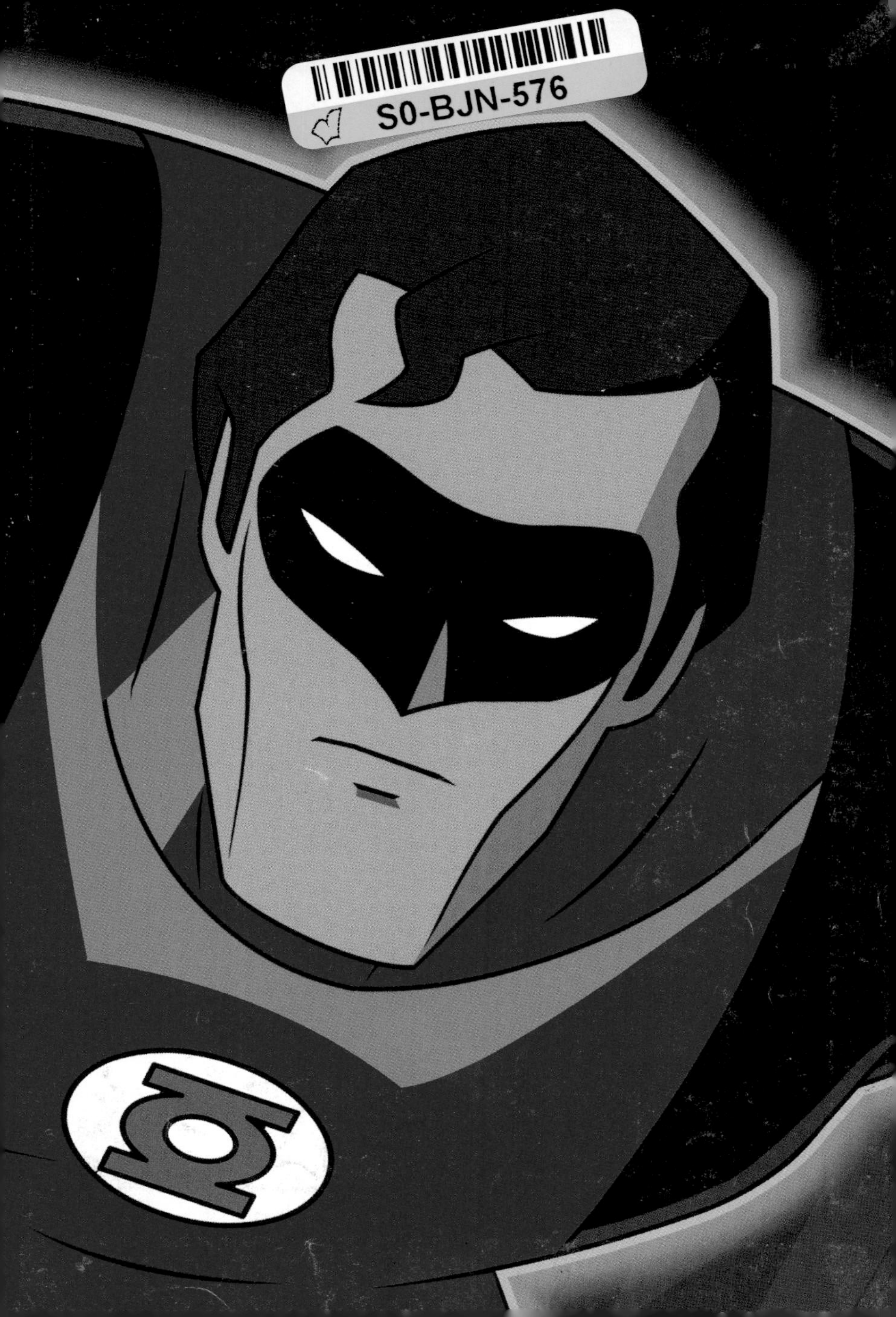

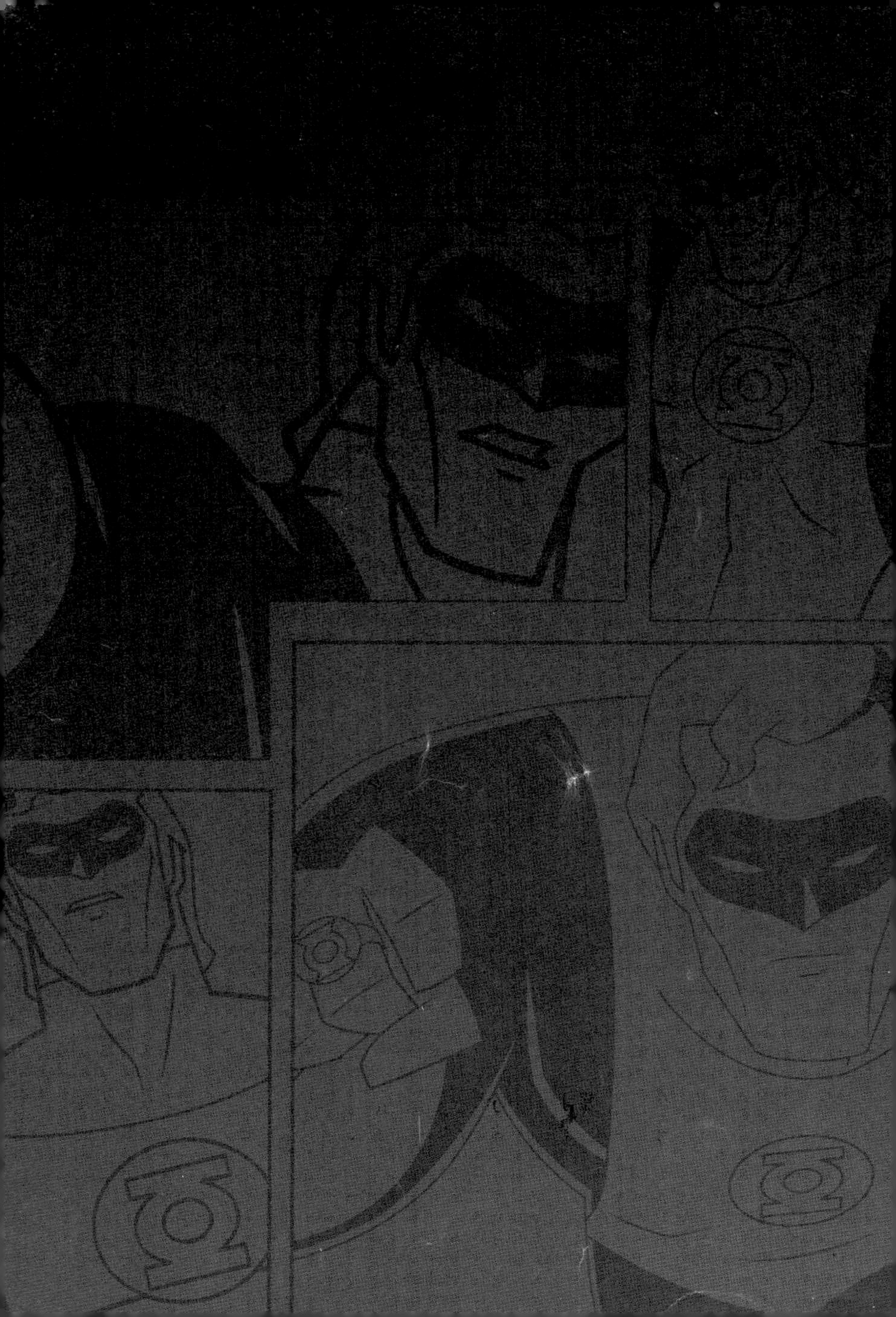

AS THE NEWEST MEMBER OF AN INTERGALACTIC PEACEKEEPING
FORCE KNOWN AS THE GREEN LANTERN CORPS, HAL JORDAN
FIGHTS EVIL AND PROUDLY WEARS THE UNIFORM AND RING OF . . .

SUPER DC HEROES
GREEN LANTERN

THE LAST SUPER HERO

WRITTEN BY
MICHAEL DAHL

ILLUSTRATED BY
DAN SCHOENING

STONE ARCH BOOKS
a capstone imprint

Published by Stone Arch Books in 2011
A Capstone Imprint
151 Good Counsel Drive, P.O. Box 669
Mankato, Minnesota 56002
www.capstonepub.com

Library of Congress Cataloging-in-Publication Data

Dahl, Michael.
    Guardian of Earth / written by Michael Dahl ; illustrated by Dan Schoening.
        p. cm. -- (DC super heroes. Green Lantern)
    ISBN 978-1-4342-2612-9 (library binding) -- ISBN 978-1-4342-3082-9 (pbk.)
    1. Graphic novels. [1. Graphic novels. 2. Superheroes--Fiction.] I. Schoening,
Dan, ill. II. Title.
    PZ7.7.D34Gu 2011
    741.5'973--dc22   2010025600

Summary: Hal Jordan of Earth is recruited to join an intergalactic law
enforcement squadron known as the Green Lanterns. He is summoned to their
headquarters on the planet Oa, which lies at the center of the universe. But
before they can finish their training, Hal, and his new teammates are caught
up in a battle that will test the very limits of their courage and willpower. A
ruthless enemy traps them on a deserted planet. The power rings of the Green
Lanterns have no effect on the alien weapons. With his companions defeated or
imprisoned, Hal must quickly learn to become a super hero before he becomes
the last.

Art Director: Bob Lentz
Designer: Hilary Wacholz
Production Specialist: Michelle Biedscheid

Printed in the United States of America in Stevens Point, Wisconsin.
092010
005934WZS11

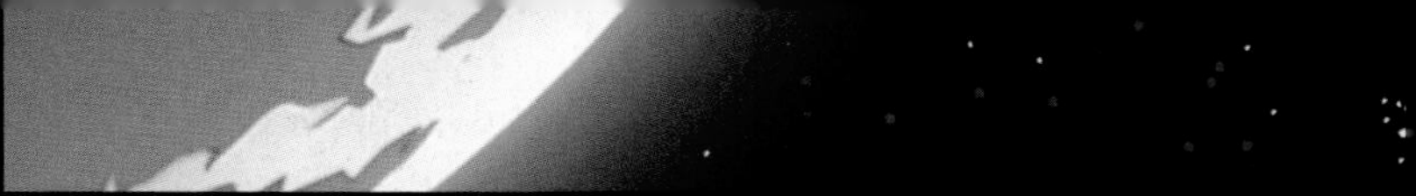

TABLE OF CONTENTS

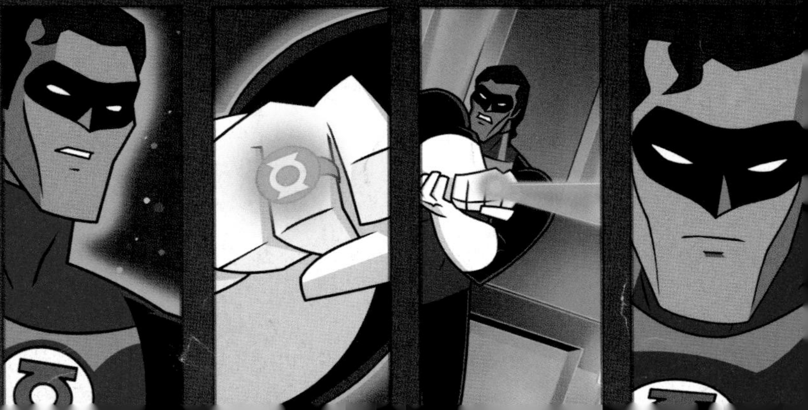

CHAPTER 1

THE POWER OF YELLOW

ZWWWoOOOOMMMM!

"This is *not* happening to me!" Hal Jordan shouted.

Jordan was flying faster than he had ever flown before. As a test pilot, he was used to breaking a speed record or the sound barrier. But this time, Hal Jordan was flying through the Milky Way Galaxy powered only by the small green ring that glowed on his right hand. A gleaming shell, created by the ring, covered his body. It protected him from the cold of outer space.

"Don't lose your concentration," came a voice at Hal's side, "or you'll lose your life."

Hal looked over at his traveling companion, a magenta-colored being known as Sinestro.

"The ring takes its orders from your mind," added Sinestro. "If your mind wanders, the ring loses focus. Don't ever forget that, Earthman."

Sinestro was a leading member of the Green Lantern Corps, a peacekeeping force that patrolled the universe by using the green power rings to fight crime. Hal had been chosen to be the Green Lantern for Sector 2814, which included planet Earth.

Hal received his ring from Abin Sur, a powerful Green Lantern whose ship had crashed on Earth after a battle.

Abin found Hal and gave him his ring. Soon afterward, the wounded warrior died. Sinestro had been sent to contact Hal and bring him back to the corps' headquarters on the planet Oa. There he would be tested and trained.

"Exactly how far away is this Oa place?" asked Hal.

"Farther than your human mind can imagine," Sinestro replied. "Oa lies at the center of the universe."

"So, what, a couple hours?" joked Hal. He knew Sinestro would not answer.

Suddenly, Sinestro shouted. "Earthman! Stay alert!"

WHOOOOSH! The warriors were swallowed by a vast nebula. Swirling streams of colorful gas surrounded them.

Hal caught a glimpse of a dark, moving mass — a meteoroid! It was heading straight toward them!

Sinestro aimed his ring at the speeding rock. A glowing green torpedo launcher grew out of his arm.  The green torpedo smashed the meteoroid into thousands of harmless pieces.

Cool, thought Hal. But he didn't have long to admire Sinestro's wits. A dozen more meteoroids tumbled toward them.

SMASH! CRUNCH! BANG!

The two Green Lanterns swatted the space rocks from their path.

Then Hal noticed a final meteoroid flying toward him. The rock had passed through a golden-colored spiral of gas and had turned bright yellow.

Hal willed a giant green flyswatter and smacked at the meteroid. **WHOOOOSH!**

But instead of striking the rock, the green flyswatter simply dissolved! "What?!" Hal cried as the meteoroid continued zooming straight toward him.

A pair of green tongs flashed from Sinestro's ring. They grabbed Hal's waist and plucked him to safety as the meteoroid rumbled past.

"What happened?" said Hal.

"Your powers are helpless against the color yellow," said Sinestro.

"*Now* you tell me!" said Hal.

"With discipline and willpower, one can learn to overcome the power of yellow," Sinestro added. "Yellow represents fear."

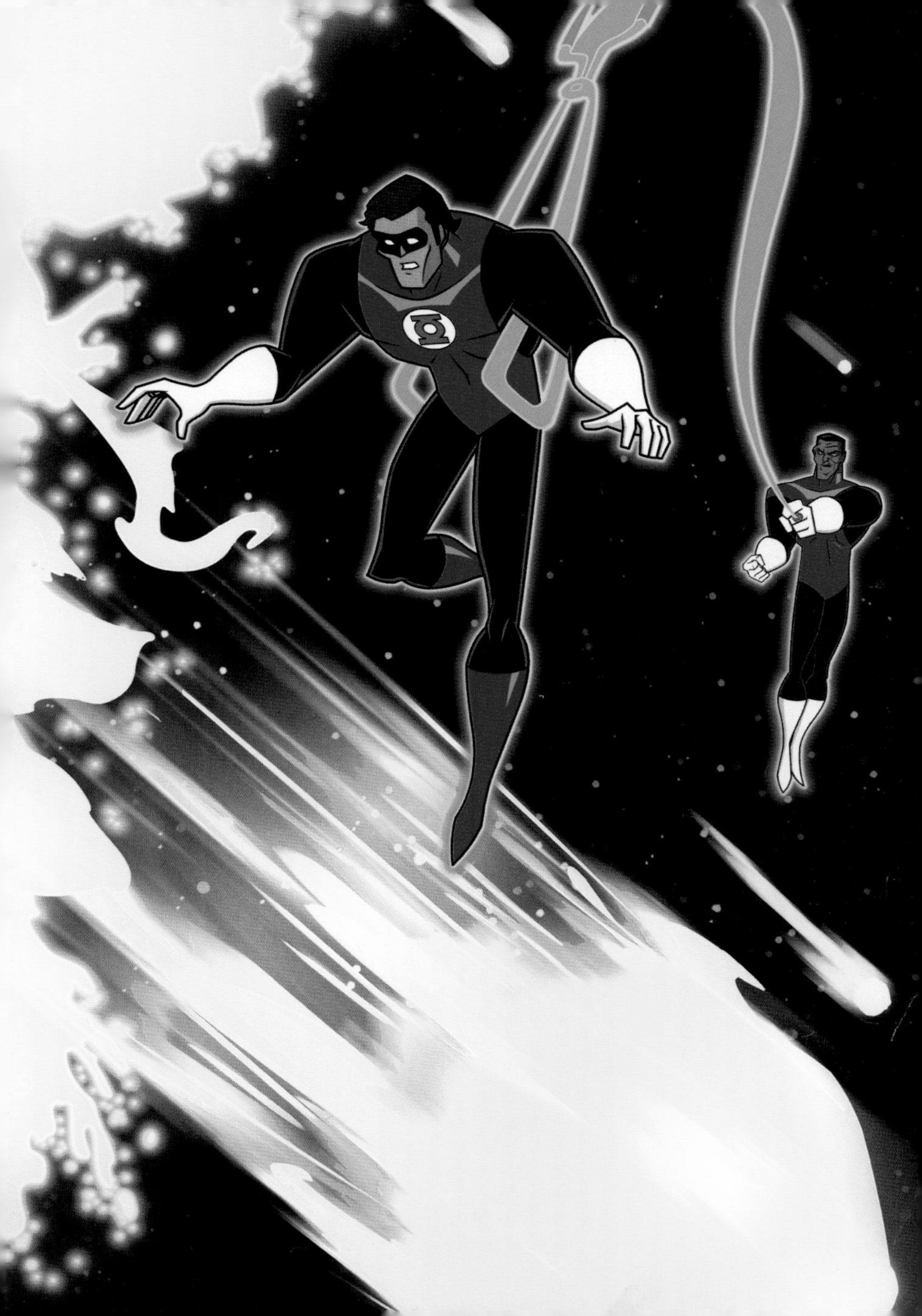

"To conquer fear," Sinestro said, "you must have great willpower and channel it through the green energy of your ring."

"Not a problem," Hal said. "Nothing scares me."

"Nothing?" asked Sinestro.

Everyone's afraid of something, Hal remembered his father had once told him. Perhaps Sinestro was right.

The two warriors burst out of the nebula and resumed their journey. They flew through dozens of patrol zones, or sectors, each one protected by a different Green Lantern. Each time they entered a new sector, the Green Lantern of that sector would greet them with a burst of light from his power ring. The lights seemed to guide them on their way to Oa.

It's like a police escort, thought Hal. "It's nice to see some team spirit," he said.

"They have not come out to greet you," said Sinestro. "They are showing respect to the memory and the ring of Abin Sur. It is a tradition whenever a Green Lantern dies."

Hal thought of the yellow meteoroid that had almost hit him. "By the way, thanks for saving my life," he said.

Sinestro, unblinking, stared straight ahead. "That is what Green Lanterns do," he said.

Oa was still trillions of light-years away, but Hal realized his training had already begun.

CHAPTER 2

GREEN RECRUIT

Long before he saw the planet, Hal saw its beacon. A huge pillar of green light surged upward from Oa's surface. Hal could see hundreds of green specks, glowing like fireflies, rushing toward or away from the beam. They were galactic warriors, wearing the same uniform as Hal and Sinestro, each one bound on a heroic mission.

Nearing the planet, Hal could see that Oa was mostly desert. The beacon came from the planet's only city — one that was larger than New York and Tokyo combined.

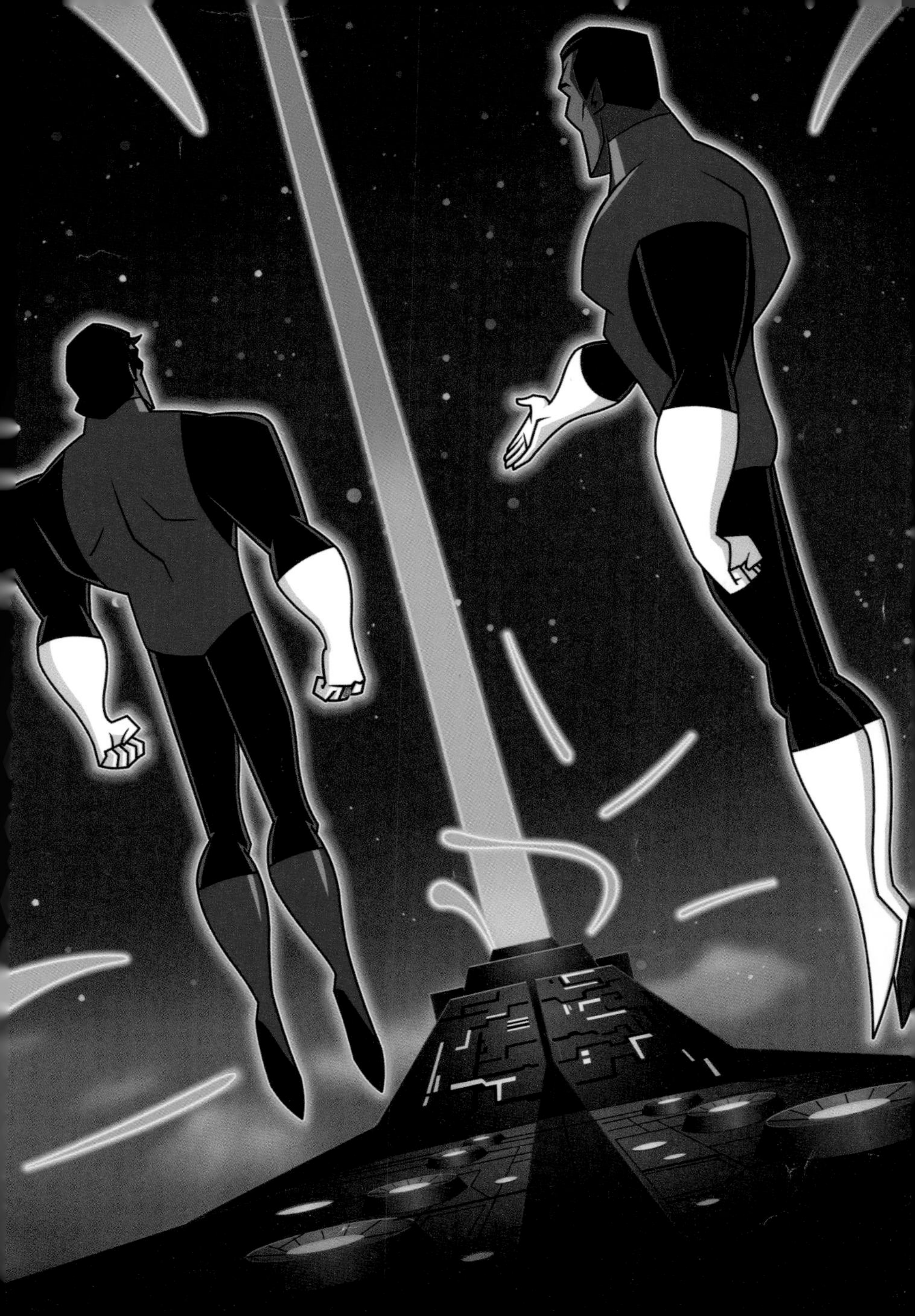

Sinestro slowed down. Hal hovered next to him.

"Don't tell me," said Hal. "We haven't been cleared for landing."

Then Hal saw two glowing specks rushing upward from the city and heading in his direction. The specks were two corps members, protected by green light-shells like Hal's.

One of the warriors was orange-skinned with a bird's beak for a mouth. A fish's fin ran down the back of his head. The other resembled a giant polished diamond. But this diamond was alive and wore a green power ring on one of its eel-like arms.

The Green Lantern with the bird beak nodded at Hal. "You wear the ring of Abin Sur," he said.

The diamond creature's tentacles whipped up and down. "We are on our way to Sector 1416," it said. "My sector. The planet Thogo is under attack. We need you, Sinestro."

Sinestro nodded toward Hal. "I was ordered to bring him here for training," he said. "Well, Earthman, I guess your training starts now!"

ZWWWOOOMMMM!

Hal and the three warriors sped off into space. By listening to Sinestro bark out orders, Hal learned the names of his new companions. The alien with the bird beak was Tomar-Tu. The diamond creature was Chaselon. Soon they arrived at a planet bathing in the light of twin suns. Hal noticed a huge fleet of starships circling the planet.

"The Qwedic are invading again," said Chaselon.

"It seems they did not learn their lesson from last time," said Sinestro.

"I shall approach the commander's ship," Tomar-Tu suggested. "Perhaps if I explain —"

A blast of green energy hurtled past Tomar-Tu and struck the Qwedic commander's ship.

The ship spun out of control toward the planet.

"Sinestro!" cried Chaselon.

"They won't forget this time," said the magenta-skinned fighter. He sent another blast at a ship on the far end of the fleet.

"That was not needed," said Tomar-Tu.

"We should destroy the fleet," said Sinestro. "This is a waste of time."

This guy's cold, thought Hal.

"There are thousands of Qwedic soldiers aboard those ships," said Chaselon.

"And millions of Thogons on the planet below," Sinestro pointed out. "Don't argue about numbers. We are here to keep the peace. So, let's keep it." Then he added, "Let's blast those who don't want peace into the next galaxy!"

Tomar-Tu and Chaselon aimed at the enemy's fuel supplies. ZZRRRRRTT! They made the ships unable to attack.

"Hal Jordan!" shouted Sinestro. "Destroy those two ships nearest you!"

Hal wasn't sure what to do. Tomar-Tu and Chaselon were looking at him. Hal knew what the two Green Lanterns were thinking. Would this Earthman use his powers the way they were using theirs? Or would Hal be as ruthless as Sinestro?

One of the Qwedic ships turned toward them. Cannons on either side of the ship shot two missiles. Hal focused. A beam of light leaped from his ring. It created a gigantic slide that caught the missiles and turned them back toward the alien ships.

The two missiles broadsided another vessel and knocked out its power supply.

"Quick thinking, Earthman," said Tomar-Tu. "You saved our lives and stopped one of the ships."

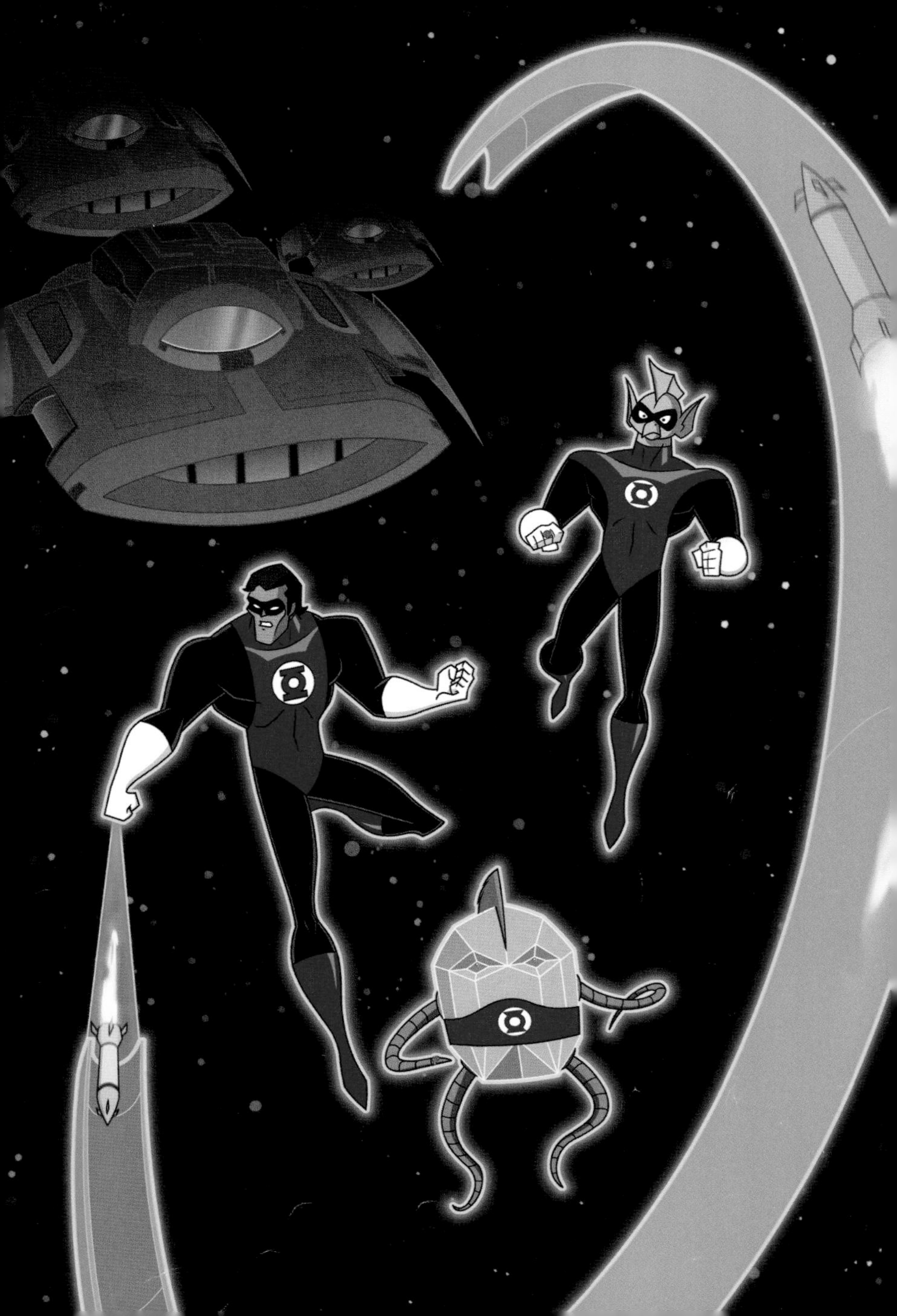

"Back home we call that killing two birds with one stone," said Hal.

"A good strategy," said Tomar-Tu.

"What is a bird?" asked Chaselon.

"We're not finished!" roared Sinestro.

The four warriors continued disabling the enemy fleet. The Qwedic weapons could not resist the power of the Green Lanterns.

Hal noticed that Sinestro had stopped trying to destroy the alien soldiers. Instead, he had quietly joined his comrades in demolishing the ships' power sources.

When all the ships were disarmed, the squad of Green Lanterns combined their energies and formed a green chain that shackled the ships together.

Then they hauled the imprisoned fleet back to its home planet of Qweda, where they left the ships circling in a harmless orbit.

"Mission accomplished!" Hal shouted. Tomar-Tu smiled. A cheerful light gleamed from one of Chaselon's facets.

"So, how did I do today, coach?" asked Hal, turning toward Sinestro.

"You disobeyed a direct order to destroy those ships," said Sinestro.

"Guess I'm still learning the ropes," said Hal. "Sorry for saving that planet."

"You Earthlings are too unpredictable," said Sinestro. He turned to Tomar-Tu and Chaselon. "Look what his kind have done to their own planet! What if I can't count on this creature to back me up?"

"Hal is doing an excellent job," said Chaselon. "I believe he has the heart of a true Green Lantern."

"Thanks, Chaz," said Hal. "I'm glad someone's on my side."

Chaselon wrapped his tentacles around the Earthman's body and squeezed.

"I'm not really a hug kind of guy," said Hal. "Wait! Hey, I can't breathe." One of Chaselon's metallic limbs change into a snake. "I am sorry," said the diamond being. "But you must be eliminated."

"What?!" shouted Tomar-Tu.

Hal looked and saw a second Chaselon hovering in front of him. Instantly, the diamond warrior threatening Hal faded into the air. The real Chaselon remained floating in front of Hal, waving his arms.

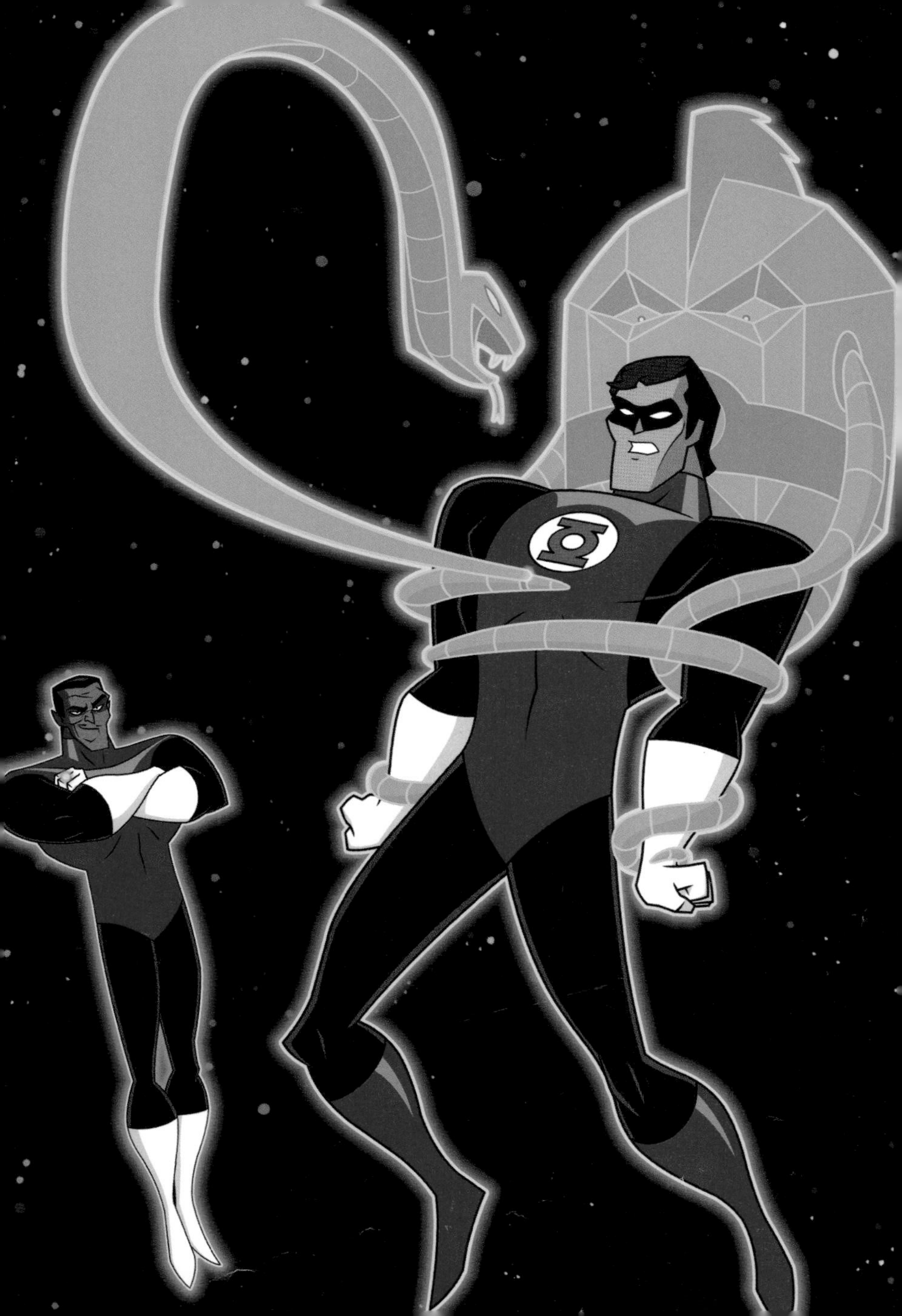

"That wasn't me," said Chaselon.

"Another trial," said Sinestro. "That was an illusion that I created. A Green Lantern must be prepared for any kind of attack. You must not allow your feelings to get the better of you. Especially the feeling of fear."

Tomar-Tu nodded his bird-like head.

Who said I was afraid? thought Hal, angrily. He suddenly remembered what Sinestro had said about the color yellow. Maybe Hal was afraid of something after all. But if that was true, it was the fear of making a mistake. The fear of failure.

"A Green Lantern cannot fail his friends," said Sinestro. Hal wondered if his trainer could read his mind.

The four soldiers then flew back to Oa.

CHAPTER 3

OUT OF THE BLUE

As Hal approached the planet Oa, he saw a shower of green comets rushing toward him and his companions.

"What's going on?" asked Chaselon.

"Bad news," said Sinestro.

The comets turned out to be a squad of Green Lanterns, young recruits from across the galaxies. They halted in front of the warriors, miles above Oa's surface.

"Z'mash, reporting for duty, Sinestro, sir," said one of the hovering recruits.

The alien was about half the size of Hal, gray-skinned, and had a set of thick, curving horns. He reminded Hal of a ram.

"We're here for the Belaquafa defense," said another who resembled a giant silver jellyfish. Electrical sparks traveled up and down its tendrils.

"Belaquafa is light-years from here," Tomar-Tu explained to Hal.

"The inhabitants of its triple moons are big trouble," added Chaselon. "The Guardians worry that the moons' armies will soon develop ultra-nuclear weapons."

"That's exactly what's happened," butted in the ram-boy, Z'mash. "Begging your pardon for the interruption, sir. But the Guardians ordered us to find you. They figured you needed back-up."

"And they figured you needed the training," finished Sinestro.

"Exactly, sir," said Z'mash, with a sheepish grin.

"That is not all," added the jellyfish creature whose name was Tendryllant. "The Guardians also picked up images of the Qwedic ships returning to attack Thogo."

"I knew it!" shouted Sinestro. "Our counter-attack was weak. We should have destroyed those ships when we had the chance. Tomar-Tu! Chaselon! You are coming with me to finish the job."

"What about the rest of us?" asked Hal.

Sinestro looked at the recruits. "Head to Belaquafa," he replied. "Let's see if you can handle a simple mission on your own."

"Green Lanterns! About face!" he said.

Sinestro and the senior Green Lanterns vanished in a blur of emerald. The squad of newer warriors flew toward Belaquafa. Hal shot a backward glance at Oa. *Will I ever land on that planet?* he wondered.

*　　*　　*

Soon, the recruits were orbiting the blue-green Belaquafa. Red beams of nuclear energy were shooting from the planet's moons. The beams burned into Belaquafa's oceans, creating tidal waves of super-heated water.

"Let's station ourselves between the moons and the planet," shouted Hal.

The warriors flew into position. They aimed their power rings at the attacking energy beams.

Z'mash was staring past his comrades. "Didn't someone say this place had *three* moons?" he asked Hal.

Hal looked around quickly. "You're right," he said. "I thought I counted three when we got here."

At that moment, the two moons faded from the sky. The red beams of destruction turned into mist.

Hal grew worried. "To the planet's surface," he said. As the squad neared Belaquafa's surface, the ocean disappeared. The tidal waves were gone. When the Green Lanterns landed on the surface, their boots stood on dry, gritty sand.

"This is definitely not Belaquafa," said Z'mash.

"The ocean was a mirage," said Hal.

Iktik, a recruit that reminded Hal of a stick insect, held up his slender fist. "Ring-ring," he commanded. "Where are we-we?"

A shower of dirt and stones flew up from the ground. A missile had crashed only a few meters away. The new recruits huddled together and used their rings to form a protective green dome.

"Look!" shouted one of them.

Hal saw another missile hissing toward them. The missile was yellow.

Hal concentrated his mind. He willed his ring to create a gigantic green shovel that scooped up his comrades, him, gravel, dome and all. He placed them safely a hundred feet away, just as the missile made landfall.

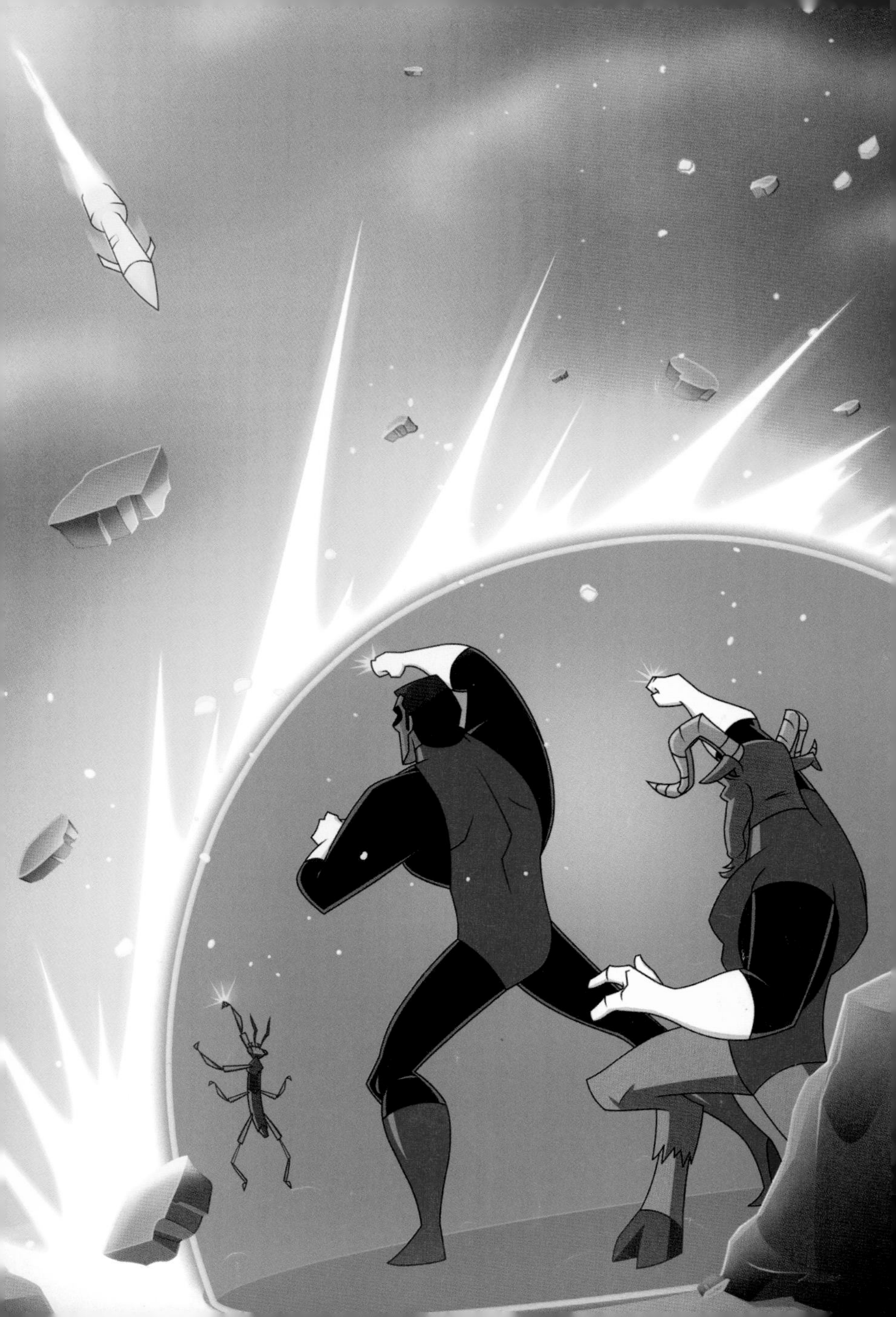

"The missile was yellow," said Z'mash. "Our dome would never have stopped that weapon."

"But it should," said Hal. "Sinestro said that our willpower can defeat yellow. We just have to learn not to fear —"

"What about those trainees that were killed on Merrikhan 5?" asked Tendryllant. "A giant yellow spider ate them!"

Hal saw fear spreading across the recruits' faces.

Iktik pointed a thin finger upward. "What-what is that-that?" he cried.

Hal looked up and saw a strange craft that looked like a massive crystal. Dozens of mirror-like sides flashed in the sunlight, each one a different color.

"This is the dawn of a new day," came a voice from the ship. "The Guardians and the Green Lantern Corps are no longer needed. We are the new guardians."

"Disturbing news," said Tendryllant.

"It's not news," said Hal. "It's garbage!"

"We are from the mirror planet, Zwawz," continued the voice. "No one in the universe can match our technology of light and images. We can create a mirage as large as a planet. Give up your rings and acknowledge us as your new masters."

"Never!" shouted Z'mash. The warrior zoomed toward the ship. Then he suddenly stopped. A mighty beam of yellow energy blasted toward the planet's surface. From another side of the ship, a dozen yellow beams shot out like searchlights.

"The sky is yellow-yellow!" cried Iktik.

"Not the sky," said Tendryllant. "It is a great dome. A force field of yellow energy is covering the entire planet."

"We're trapped!" shouted Z'mash, still hovering in the air.

Hal looked at the squad of new recruits. Their eyes were growing wide with terror.

"Your rings are useless here," said the voice from the ship. "We know the weakness of the Green Lantern Corps — the color yellow, the color of fear."

A beam of light shot down from the ship and a shape rose from the ground. A giant yellow spider reared up on its monstrous legs. Several of the recruits fled in terror. Then Hal heard Z'mash scream and saw him fall toward the ground.

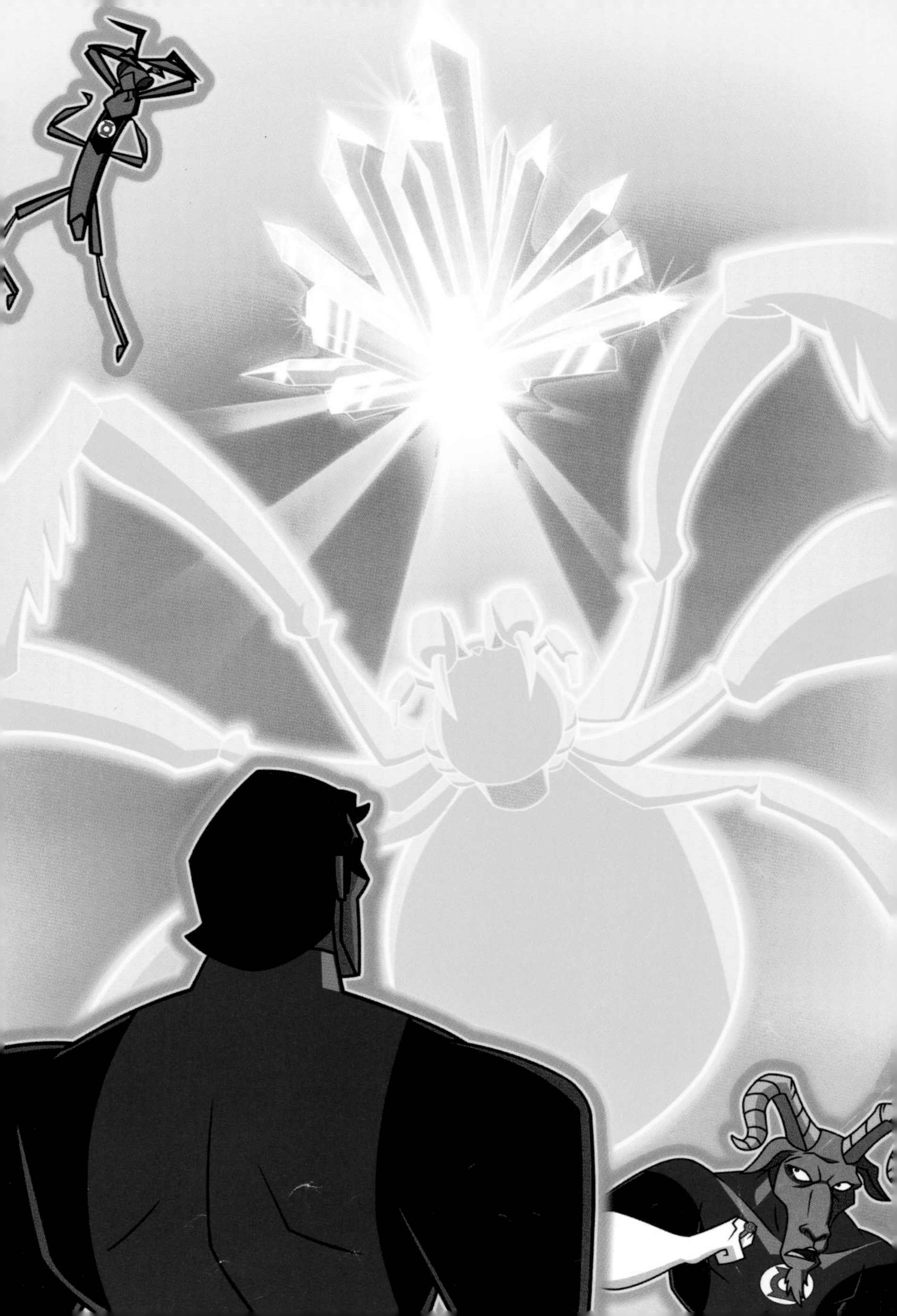

CHAPTER 4

A BLACK DAY

Hal Jordan commanded his ring to create an airplane's pilot seat to catch the falling ram-boy. Hal rushed to his side. "I am fine, sir," said Z'mash.

BOOM! Another blast from the ship flashed above their heads. The invaders from Zwawz were waging a full attack.

The recruits ran for cover. The giant yellow spider roared and lunged at them.

"It's a mirage!" shouted Hal. "Don't give in to your fear!"

Tendryllant rallied a group of frightened recruits. They merged the beams from their rings. The combined strength of their weapons launched at the spider.

The spider vanished, just as another energy blast from the ship crashed into the ground. Dozens of emerald warriors were hurled off their feet.

Hal Jordan looked at his ring. "Power levels at sixty percent," it said.

"That better be enough," said Hal. He raised his fist and flew straight toward the weird ship.

"Ah, a new species," said the Zwawz speaker. "I believe you are the first Earth creature we have encountered."

"And let me be the last!" said Hal.

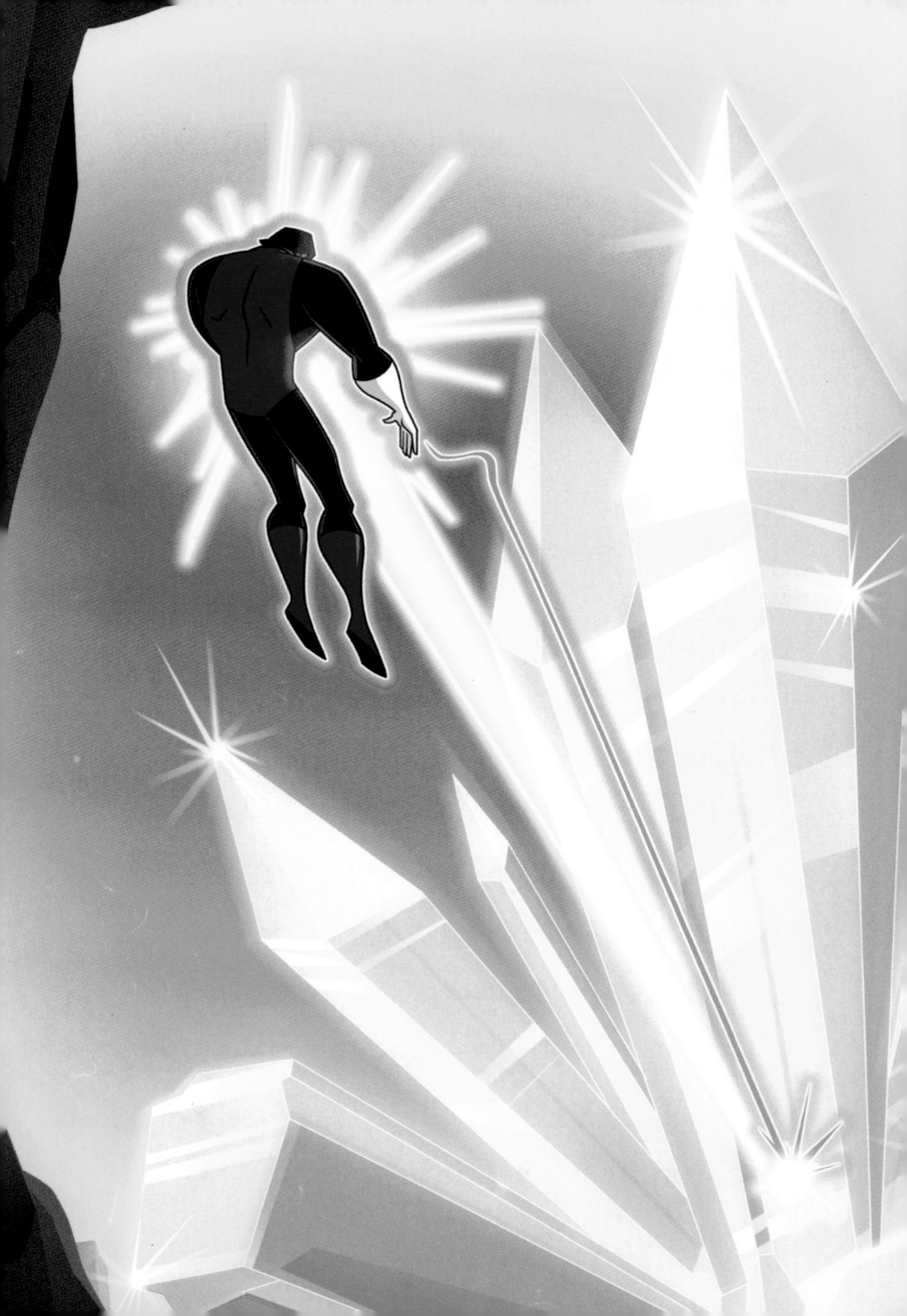

The super hero willed a green laser that struck the side of the alien ship. But the ship's crystal sides worked like prisms. They changed the wavelength of Hal's green beam and turned it yellow. The golden beam bounced back from the ship and flashed toward Hal's chest.

The Earthman had only a nanosecond to focus his willpower. He imagined a thick barrier between himself and the ship. But it wasn't enough. The force of the attack flung Hal down and backward through crumbling cliffs and mountains of rock.

A voice vibrated from the crystal ship. "You will indeed be the last, Earthman," it said. "The very last!"

Hal slumped face down onto the gravel. "I will not give up," he told himself. "No color can be stronger than a person's will."

The crystal ship landed on the planet's surface. A squadron of armed robots marched out. They rounded up the weak and dazed Green Lanterns, shoving them into yellow metal cages.

"After we cage them all," said one of the robots, "we shall strike at their home planet, Oa. This squad has shown us how weak they really are."

Hal watched this scene from a distance. The impact of the ship's beam had hurled him far away from his comrades. He wondered if the robots would notice him.

Hal saw one of the robots pointing in his direction. "Over there!" it said. "On the ground. He's the last super hero."

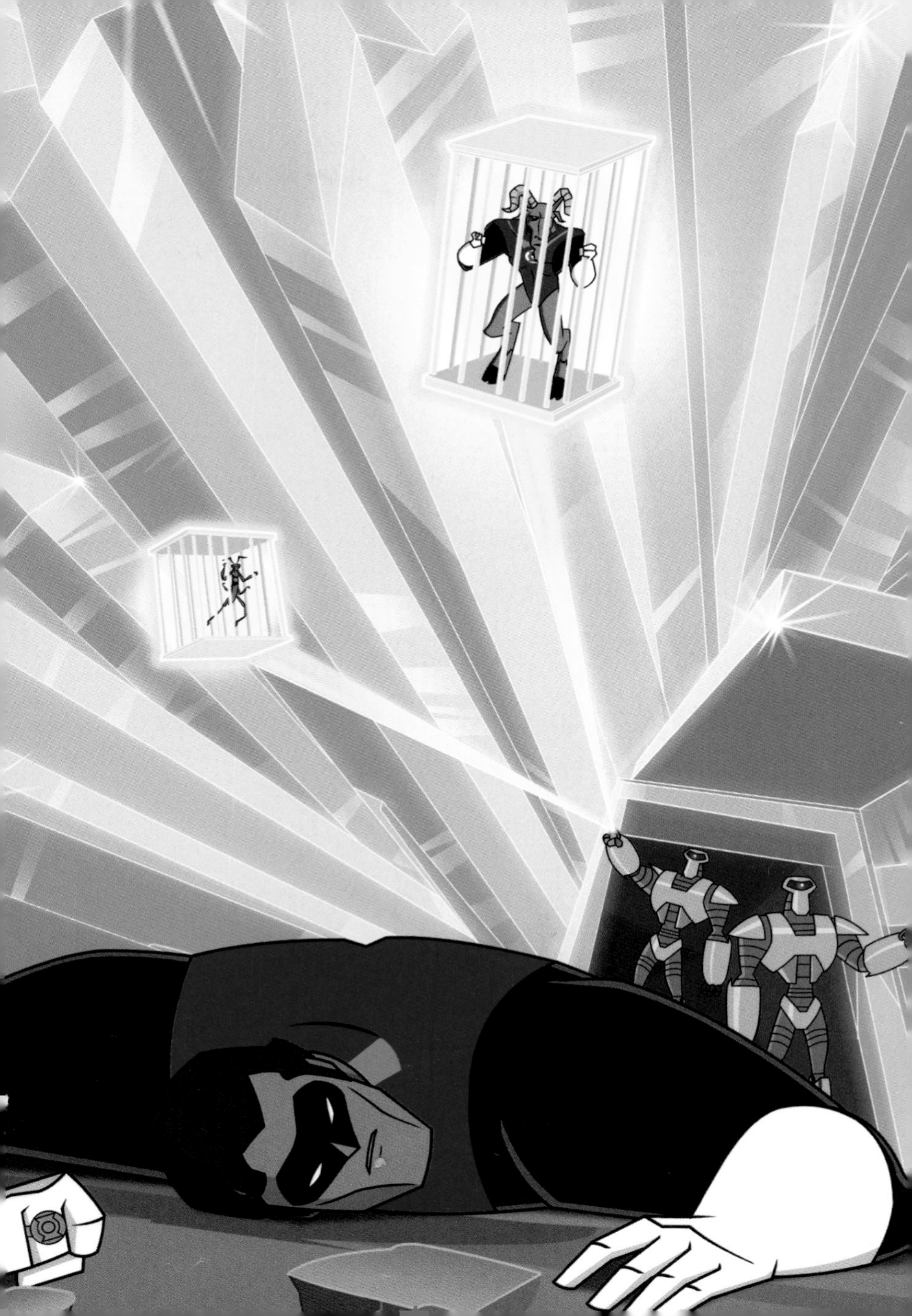

CHAPTER 5

FLYING COLORS

Hal stood and pointed back at the robots. "You're not putting me in your cage," he cried.

The robot aimed a weapon at Hal. "You cannot resist," replied the robot.

"Oh yes, I can," said Hal. "That is exactly what I'm doing. Resisting."

The speakers from the crystal ship snapped on. "Surrender, Earthman," came the Zwawz voice. "Your powers are useless against the color yellow."

"You can't scare me with the color yellow," said Hal. "Oh, you might scare others, but that's all you're doing. Trying to make them afraid. Afraid of dying, or afraid of failing. But there's something more powerful than fear." Hal grinned. "And that's simple stubbornness."

He used his ring to create a giant green toucan bird to bite open the bars of the yellow cage nearest him. "In other words," added Hal, "willpower!"

Z'mash stood up inside a cage that was being craned into the crystal ship. Hal saw a smile on the ram-boy's face. "No need to bite the bars off my cage," shouted Z'mash.

He passed easily through the bars of his prison, flew through the air, and landed beside Hal. "Shoulder to shoulder," said Z'mash. "We fight unafraid."

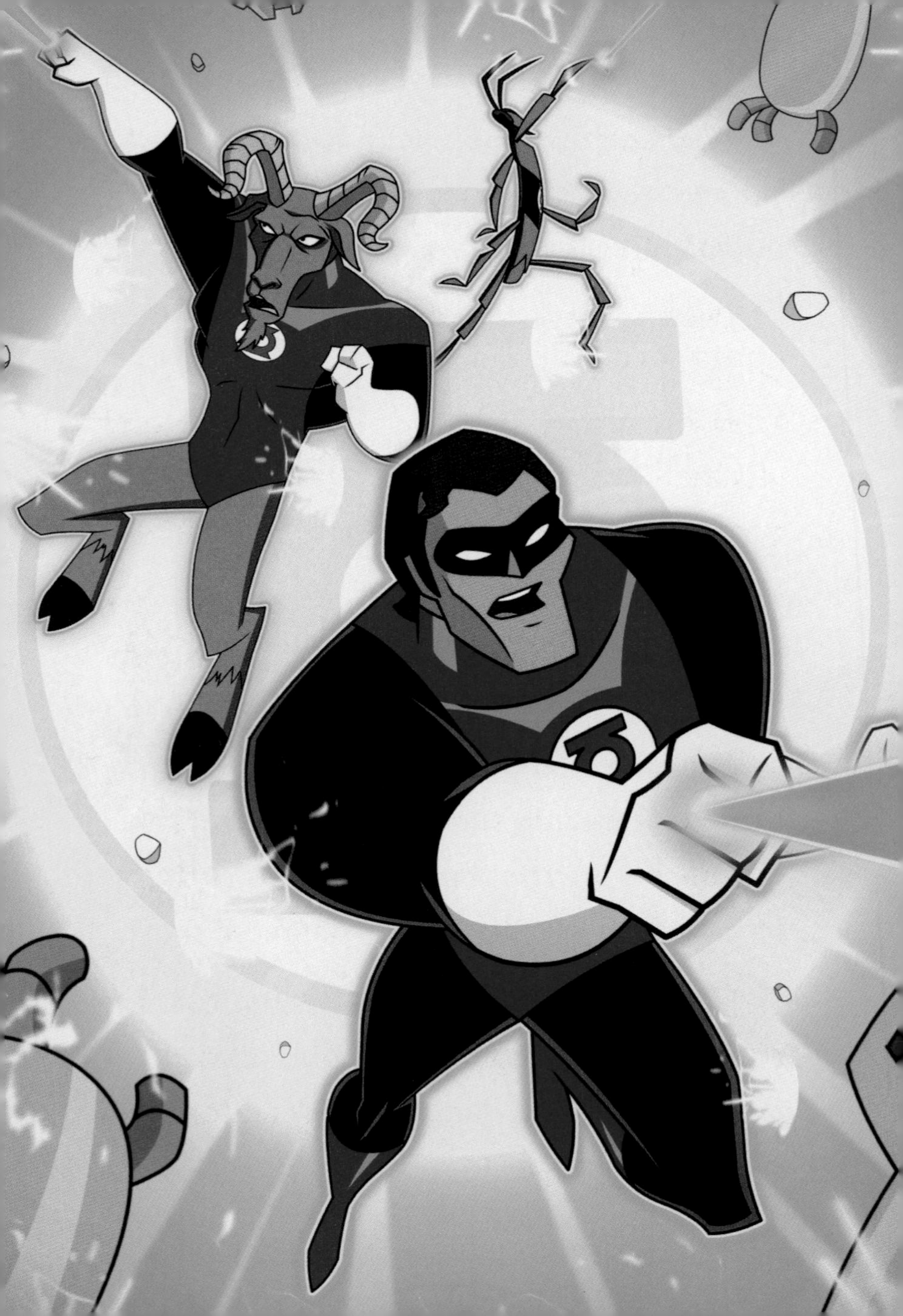

With each new Green Lantern freed, the emerald warriors grew more and more powerful. **BANG! SMASH!**

One by one, the recruits reduced the battle robots to heaps of melting scrap. They whooped and shouted with each new victory. They almost couldn't believe their eyes as they defeated every yellow weapon the aliens hurled at them.

Soon the crystal ship was surrounded by the emerald warriors. "Now it is your turn to surrender," said Hal. He aimed a green blast at the ship's power source. There was a single loud explosion, and then the ship's mirrored sides grew dark and still.

"It truly is the dawn of a new-new day," said Iktik. "But not-not for the Zwawz."

"Look up there!" said Tendryllant.

Sinestro and the senior Green Lanterns descended through the atmosphere.

"Don't tell me," said Hal. "But the fleet of Qwedic ships was a mirage."

Tomar-Tu nodded as he landed beside Hal. "Indeed, it was an illusion," he replied.

"A waste of time," added Chaselon.

Sinestro stared at the blast pits in the ground made by the Zwawz weapons. He noticed that a few recruits were tending to wounded comrades. Then he glanced at the disabled crystal ship. He nodded his head. "The Qwedic were a diversion," he said.

"A dangerous diversion," said Hal. He explained the battle against the ship and the illusions of the Zwawz.

"Hal Jordan showed us how to fight against our fear," said Z'mash.

"The color yellow holds no power over us," said Iktik.

"Never again!" shouted the recruits.

"I will have to report this to the Guardians," said Sinestro.

"You will also report how well the recruits did under fire," said Tomar-Tu. He put his hand on Hal's shoulder. "You especially, Hal Jordan."

"You helped save our lives," said Tendryllant.

"It's what Green Lanterns do," said Hal.

Chaselon beamed. "Abin Sur would have been proud," he added.

Hal looked up at the planet's sky. The yellow dome had vanished. The stars were visible overhead.

"I'm proud of all of us," said Hal. "We're quite a team. And I'd say we passed our training with flying colors!"

Sinestro gathered the warriors around him. "We've used much energy today," he said. "Let's power up and return home."

The warriors cheered.

Finally, I'll get to Oa, thought Hal.

Sinestro produced a green power battery. All the warriors lifted their rings to it and chanted together . . .

In brightest day,
In blackest night,
No evil shall escape my sight.
Let those who worship evil's might,
Beware my power —
Green Lantern's light!

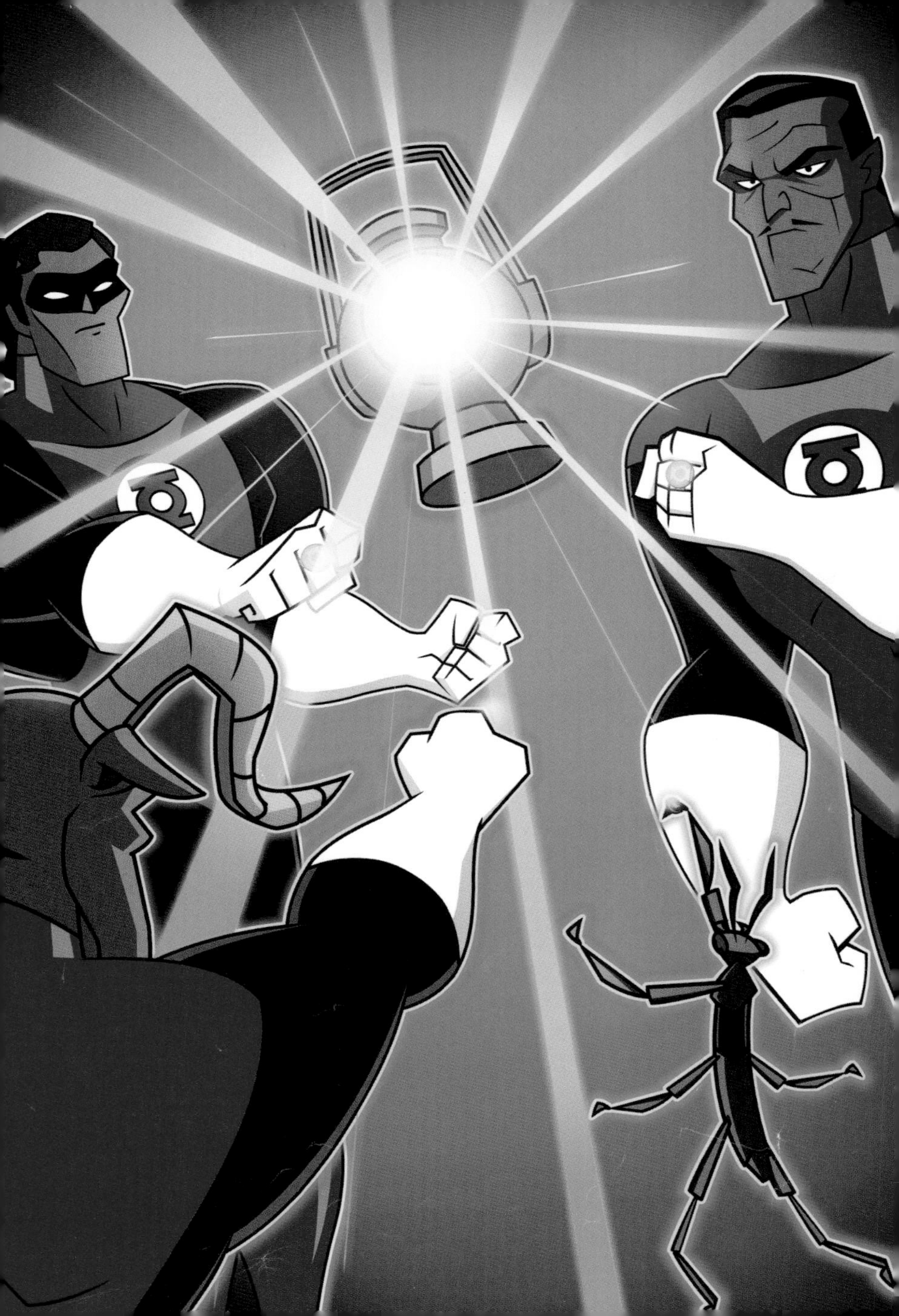

SINESTRO

BIRTHPLACE: Korugar

OCCUPATION: Green Lantern

HEIGHT: 6' 7"   **WEIGHT:** 205 lbs.

EYES: Black   **HAIR:** Black

POWERS/ABILITIES: Brilliant military commander; ring creates hard-light constructs of anything imaginable; unmatched power.

BIOGRAPHY

Born on the planet Korugar, Thaal Sinestro was appointed the Green Lantern of Sector 1417 at an early age. Soon, he became one of the most powerful members of the entire corps. He mentored many rookie members of the Green Lanterns, including Hal Jordan. Although effective, his strict leadership style and fiendish imagination drew criticism. Unwilling to change, Sinestro's loyalty to the green power ring soon turned to hatred. He eventually left the Green Lanterns, donned a yellow ring, and formed his own Sinestro Corps.

2814

Each Green Lantern patrols a specific area of space called a sector. Sinestor guarded Sector 1417, which included his home planet, Korugar.

Sinestro is the brother-in-law of Abin Sur, the Green Lantern who gave Hal Jordan his ring.

Sinestro married Arin Sur, the sister of Abin Sur. Together, they had a child named Soranik Natu. She became a powerful member of the Green Lanterns.

Sinestro used his power ring to take control of his home planet. When the Guardians of the Universe found out, they banished the former Green Lantern to the planet Qward in the Antimatter Universe.

BIOGRAPHIES

Michael Dahl is the author of more than 200 books for children and young adults. He has won the AEP Distinguished Achievement Award three times for his non-fiction. His Finnegan Zwake mystery series was shortlisted twice by the Agatha awards. He has also written the Library of Doom series and the Dragonblood books. He is a featured speaker at conferences around the country. He has written other origin stories for the DC Super Heroes series, including *The Last Son of Krypton, The Man Behind the Mask,* and *Trial of the Amazons.*

Dan Schoening was born in Victoria, B.C., Canada. From an early age, Dan has had a passion for animation and comic books. Currently, Dan does freelance work in the animation and game industry and spends a lot of time with his lovely little daughter, Paige.

GLOSSARY

beacon (BEE-kuhn)—a light or fire used as a signal or warning

comrade (KOM-rad)—a companion in combat

guardian (GAR-dee-uhn)—someone who guards or protects something

illusion (i-LOO-zhuhn)—something that appears to exist but does not

meteoroid (MEE-tee-ur-royd)—a piece of rock or metal traveling through space at high speed

mirage (muh-RAZH)—something that a person believes to see in the distance but isn't really there

nebula (NEB-yuh-luh)—a bright cloud of stars, gases, and dust that can be seen in the night sky

recruit (ri-KROOT)—someone who has recently joined an army or other organization

tradition (truh-DISH-uhn)—the handing down of customs, ideas, and beliefs from one generation to the next

willpower (WIL-pou-ur)—the ability to control what you will and will not do

DISCUSSION QUESTIONS

1. Who do you think is a better Green Lantern — Hal Jordan or Sinestro? Explain your answer.

2. Sinestro's test put Hal and the other Green Lanterns in danger. Do you think this decision was okay? Why or why not?

3. If you could travel to any planet in the solar system, where would you go? Why?

WRITING PROMPTS

1. Write another Green Lantern adventure! Where will Hal and the Corps go next? What villain will they take on?

2. Green Lanterns have unmatched willpower, the ability to control what they will and will not do. Write about three things that you must use willpower to avoid. Do you crave candy? Are video games hard to resist? Describe.

3. The Green Lantern ring can create anything the wearer imagines. If you had a ring, what would you imagine it to create? Write about your creation, and then draw a picture of it.

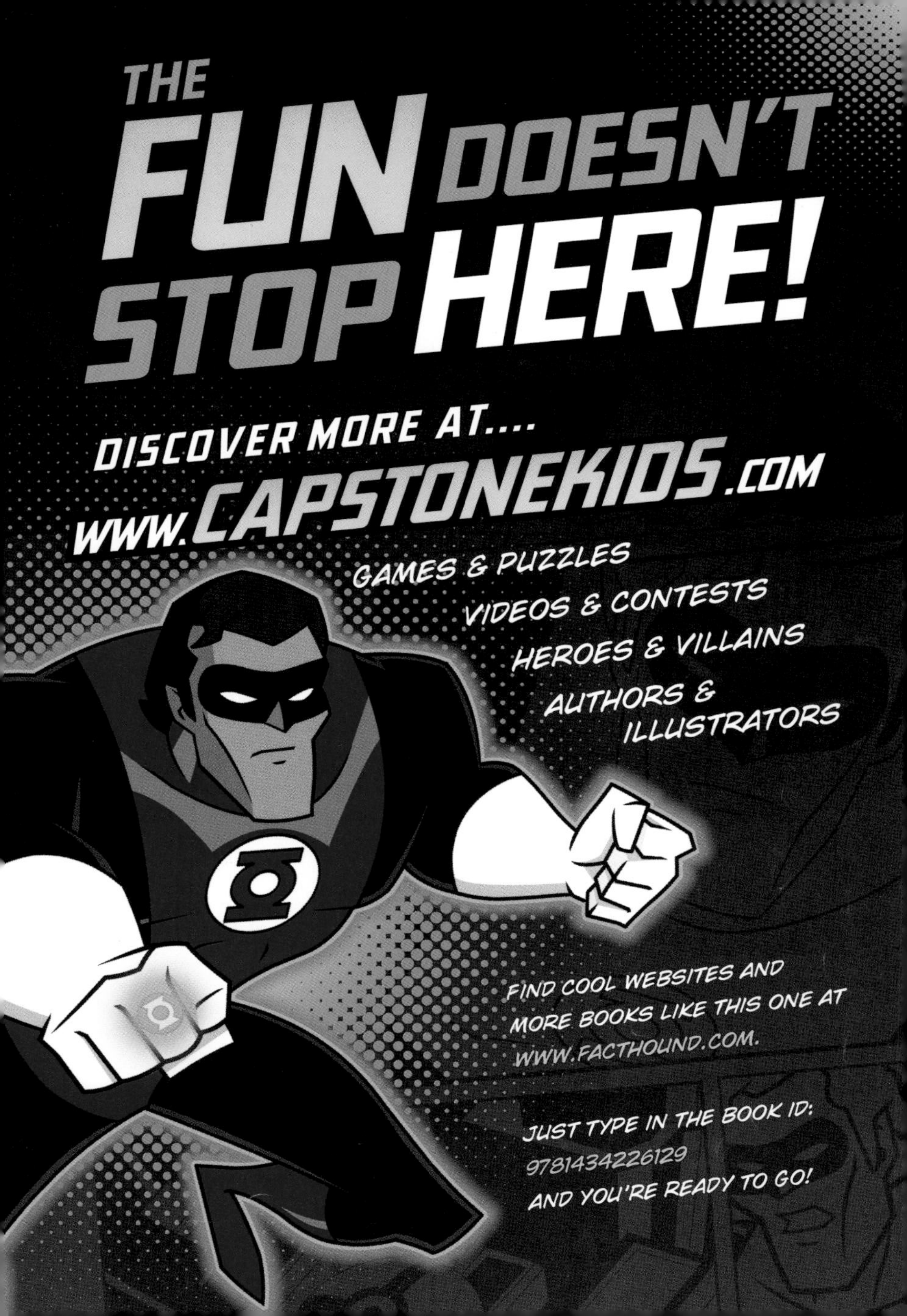
THE FUN DOESN'T STOP HERE!
DISCOVER MORE AT....
WWW.CAPSTONEKIDS.COM
GAMES & PUZZLES
VIDEOS & CONTESTS
HEROES & VILLAINS
AUTHORS & ILLUSTRATORS
FIND COOL WEBSITES AND MORE BOOKS LIKE THIS ONE AT WWW.FACTHOUND.COM.
JUST TYPE IN THE BOOK ID:
9781434226129
AND YOU'RE READY TO GO!

MORE NEW
GREEN LANTERN
VENTURES!

BEWARE OUR POWER.

TLE OF THE BLUE LANTERNS

THE LIGHT KING STRIKE

HIGH-TECH TERROR

GUARDIAN OF EARTH